BIG HAIR, DON'T CARE

Goldest Karat Publishing
P.O. Box 724621
Atlanta, GA 31139

Find more books like this at www.goldestkarat.com.

Illustrated by Megan Bair, http://www.mbaircreative.com/

This book is dedicated to every little boy and girl around the world whose hair is just a bit "different".

I've got big hair and I don't care
And even though the kids may stare
I lift my hands up in the air
Then smile and say…

I love my hair!

I've got big hair, my friend does too
And at the movies and the zoo
It often blocks out all the view
So never sit behind us two!

Sometimes I lose at hide and seek

But hair like this is so unique

Braids

Twists

And puffs are all so chic

My hair is different every week

I've got big hair and just for fun
I put my dog's hair in a bun

And then we go out for a run
And laugh and play out in the sun

My hair is big and full of flair
It's like a fancy hat I wear
So sit behind me if you dare
Oh how I really love my hair!

I've got big hair and I'm so proud
It's soft and fluffy like a cloud
And even when it's really loud
You can still find me in a crowd

My hair looks like a cotton ball
And though I'm short it makes me tall
You'll see me walking down the hall
Bookbag and books
Big hair and all

I've got big hair and I don't care
And even though the kids may stare
I lift my hands up in the air
Then smile and say I love my hair!

The End

CPSIA information can be obtained
at www.ICGtesting.com
Printed in the USA
LVOW06*2327200317
527892LV00015B/29/P